BLACKDOG
LEVI PINFOLD

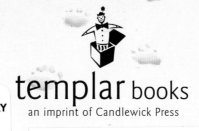

templar books
an imprint of Candlewick Press

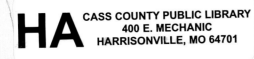

 One day, a black dog came to visit the Hope family. Mr. Hope was the first to see it.

"My goodness!" he cried, dropping his toast. He didn't waste any time in calling the police.

"There's a black dog the size of a tiger outside my house!" he told the policeman.

The policeman laughed.

"What should I do?" asked Mr. Hope.

"Don't go outside," said the policeman, and put down the phone.

Mrs. Hope was next to get up.

"My goodness!" she cried, dropping her mug of tea. She didn't waste any time in calling for Mr. Hope.

"Did you know there's a black dog the size of an elephant outside?" she yelled.

"Yes," said Mr. Hope.

"What should we do?" asked Mrs. Hope.

"Turn out the lights so it doesn't know we're here!" said Mr. Hope.

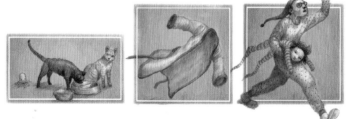

Adeline Hope was next to get up.

"My goodness!" she cried, dropping her toothbrush. She didn't waste any time in calling for her parents.

"Did you know there's a black dog the size of a *Tyrannosaurus rex* outside?"

"Yes," said Mr. and Mrs. Hope together.

"What should we do?" asked Adeline.

"Close the curtains so it can't see us."

Maurice Hope was next to get up.

"My goodness!" he cried, dropping his teddy bear. He didn't waste any time in calling for the family.

"Did you know there's a black dog the size of a Big Jeffy outside?"

"What's a Big Jeffy?" asked Adeline Hope.

"Never mind that! What should we do?" demanded Maurice Hope.

"Hide under the covers!" they all wailed.

 It was then that the youngest member of the Hope family, called Small (for short), noticed that there was something going on.

"What are you all doing under there?"

"We're hiding from the black dog!" they whispered.

"Oh, you are such sillies," said Small, opening the front door.

"Don't go out there!" cried her family.

"The hound will eat you up!"

"It'll munch your head!"

"It'll crunch your bones!"

But Small went anyway.

Outside, the Black Dog leaned
down toward her and BREATHED.
   "Golly, you ARE big!"
said Small. "What are you
doing here, you guffin?"
   The Black Dog
SNUFFED
at her.

 "All right, then," she said. "If you're going to eat me, you'll have to catch me first." And with that, she scurried into the lowering trees. As she ran, she made up a song:

"You can't follow where I go,
 unless you shrink, or don't you know?"
 The black dog followed. . . .

 As Small hurried toward the frozen pond,
under the little bridge, and over the ice, she sang:

*"Your paws are thick; ice is thin.
A great big dog just might fall in."*
And the black dog followed. . . .

 Next she scuttled through the playground, down the slide,
and around the merry-go-round, singing:

"You might be big, I may be small,
but I'm not afraid of you at all."
And still the black dog followed. . . .

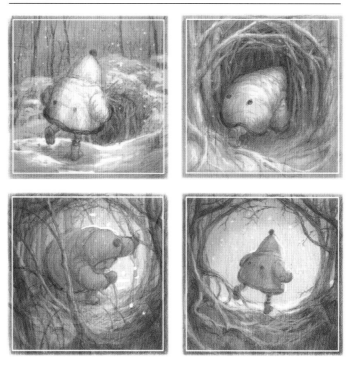

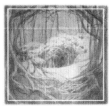 Finally, Small had run all the way back to the house.

"You'll find out why they all hide, if you follow me inside."

And with that, Small tumbled into her warm home through the cat flap. She really was that small.

And so, by now, was the black dog.

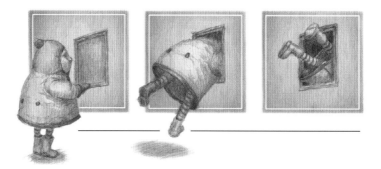

Inside, Small grabbed a laundry basket, and, as the black dog scrabbled in behind her, she covered him with a loud "HA!"

Just then, the rest of the Hope family popped up from behind their barricade.

"You haven't been munched!" cried Mrs. Hope.

"You haven't been crunched!" cheered Mr. Hope.

"You haven't been eaten!" yelled Maurice Hope (missing a poetic opportunity).

"But where's the black dog?" asked Adeline.

Without a word, Small lifted the basket.

 The rest of the Hope family was extremely pleased to see that the black dog was neither as huge nor as scary as they had feared.

"He doesn't seem fierce at all, now that I really look at him," said Mr. Hope. The rest of the family agreed.

"We were silly," said Adeline. "Only Small knew the right thing to do."
Everyone was quiet for a while, thinking about how brave Small had been.
"You've got a lot of courage, facing up to a big, fearsome thing like
that," said Mrs. Hope.

 "There was nothing to be scared of, you know," replied Small Hope as she went to sit by the fire.

And the black dog followed.